CROC NEEDS TO WAIT

A book about PATIENCE

Written by Sue Graves

Illustrated by Trevor Dunton

W
FRANKLIN WATTS
LONDON • SYDNEY

Croc was very impatient. On the day of Giraffe's birthday party, she kept asking her mum if it was time to go yet. But her mum said she would just have to **be patient and wait**!

On Monday, Miss Bird asked everyone what they had done at the weekend. She said they had to take turns to speak.

But Croc was **too excited** to wait her turn.
She **kept interrupting**. Miss Bird got cross.
She said it was rude to interrupt someone when
they were speaking.

In the maths lesson, Miss Bird told everyone to add up their sums carefully. She told them **not to rush**.

But Croc loved doing sums. She wanted to see how fast she could do them. She **forgot** to add them up carefully and she got them **all wrong**!

9

At playtime it was raining. Everyone had to stay inside and play board games. Croc loved board games. But she got **too impatient** to wait her turn.

When it was Monkey's turn, Croc grabbed the dice instead. Worse still, she knocked over the board by accident. Everyone was cross with Croc for **spoiling the game**.

After playtime Miss Bird asked Croc and Hippo to colour in a picture. Hippo coloured really carefully. He kept in the edges. But Croc was impatient to finish the picture. She didn't keep in the edges at all.

Miss Bird said it **was not neat enough** to go on the wall. Hippo was upset. He said Croc should have been more patient.

The next day Miss Bird said they were going to make clay pots for their parents. She said they must **make them carefully**. She said they must **wait** for the pots **to dry** before painting them.

But Croc was so pleased to be making a pot for her mum that she didn't take her time. She **rushed it**. Her pot ended up a very odd shape.

Croc **didn't wait** for the pot to dry before she painted it. All the paint ran off the pot and made a mess. Croc was sad.

Croc went to see Miss Bird. Miss Bird asked her
what she should have done. Croc thought about it.
She said she should have **taken her time**.
She said she should have **been patient**.
She said she should have waited for
the pot to dry before she painted it.

Miss Bird said it was better to be patient and careful than to rush and spoil things. Croc said she would try to be patient in future.

That afternoon Miss Bird said they were all going to make model boats to sail on the school pond. She said they had to work **in pairs**. Croc wanted to work with Hippo. Hippo was worried. He said Croc had to **work carefully**. Croc promised that she would.

Miss Bird gave everyone the instructions to read.
She said they had to **take turns** to do each job.

Croc and Hippo worked really hard.
Croc tried hard to be patient. She read
the instructions carefully to Hippo.

She sorted out the wooden
shapes carefully.

She **waited patiently** while Hippo glued the shapes together.

They **both waited patiently** for the glue to dry.

Then Croc painted the boat. She **took her time** and painted it really well. She and Hippo waited for the paint to dry.

Last of all, Croc waited patiently while Hippo put the sail on the boat.

Everyone took their boats to the pond. All the boats sailed well. But Croc's and Hippo's boat sailed the best of all. Croc was very pleased. She told Miss Bird that it was much better to be patient than to rush things and spoil them. Hippo said it was much nicer to work with someone who was patient!

A note about sharing this book

The *Behaviour Matters* series has been developed to provide
a starting point for further discussion on children's
behaviour both in relation to themselves and others.
The series is set in the jungle with animal
characters reflecting typical behaviour
traits often seen in young children.

Croc Needs to Wait
This story looks at the importance of being patient and realising that it is
important to take time to do things carefully and to work cooperatively
with others.

How to use the book
The book is designed for adults to share with either an individual child,
or a group of children, and as a starting point for discussion.

The book also provides visual support and repeated words and phrases
to build reading confidence.

Before reading the story
Choose a time to read when you and the children are relaxed and have
time to share the story.

Spend time looking at the illustrations and talk about what the book
might be about before reading it together.

Encourage children to employ a phonics first approach to tackling
new words by sounding the words out.

After reading, talk about the book with the children:

- Talk about the story with the children. Encourage them to retell the events in chronological order.

- Talk about Croc's impatience. Have the children felt impatient for their own birthdays to come round? Do they feel that time seems to pass too slowly when they are waiting for something exciting to happen?

- Discuss the importance of waiting their turn when others are speaking. Why should they not interrupt others? How do they feel if someone interrupts them when they are trying to explain something?

- Do the children think that Croc means to be rude or is her impatience often the result of being overexcited?

- Discuss the section of the story where Croc and Hippo work cooperatively to complete a task. Why is it important to work well with others? Can the children identify with this? Have they worked with a friend on a task? Invite them to share their experiences with the others.

- Place the children into pairs. Provide a colouring picture for each pair to complete. Tell them that they must decide which person will colour each section. Remind them that they must work cooperatively and carefully to colour the picture to the best of their abilities.

- Invite each pair to show their finished pictures to the others. Ask each pair how they decided who should colour which section and why. Ask the children to talk about sharing a task with a friend. What did they particularly enjoy about it?

29

For Isabelle, William A, William G, George, Max, Emily,
Leo, Caspar, Felix, Tabitha, Phoebe and Harry – S.G.

First published in Great Britain in 2018
by The Watts Publishing Group

Series Editor: Jackie Hamley
Series Designer: Cathryn Gilbert

A CIP catalogue record for this book is
available from the British Library.

ISBN 978 1 4451 6982 8 (paperback)

Printed in China

Franklin Watts
An imprint of
Hachette Children's Group
Part of The Watts Publishing Group
Carmelite House
50 Victoria Embankment
London EC4Y 0DZ

Hachette Ireland
8 Castlecourt
Castleknock
Dublin 15
Ireland

An Hachette UK Company
www.hachette.co.uk

www.franklinwatts.co.uk